Written by deaf children with

Julia Donaldson

Illustrated by

Nick Sharratt

What the Jackdaw Saw

MACMILLAN CHILDREN'S BOOKS

The jackdaw flew over the seaside
And this is what the jackdaw saw:

Waves crashing,
Children splashing,
Starfish sleeping,
Dolphins leaping . . .

And an octopus
touching his head with a tentacle.

"Come to my party!" the jackdaw said,
But the octopus went on touching his head.

The jackdaw flew over the farm
And this is what the jackdaw saw:

Piglets squeaking,
A gate creaking,
Cows grazing,
Sheepdog lazing . . .

And a white horse
touching her head with her hoof.

"Come to my party!" the jackdaw said,
But the horse just went on touching her head.

The jackdaw flew over the town
And this is what the jackdaw saw:

Buses rumbling,
People grumbling,
A taxi hooting,
Children scooting . . .

And a black cat
touching his head with his paw.

The jackdaw flew over a forest
And this is what the jackdaw saw:

A ferret dancing,
A deer prancing,
A fox jumping,
A rabbit thumping . . .

And a red squirrel touching her
head with her tail.

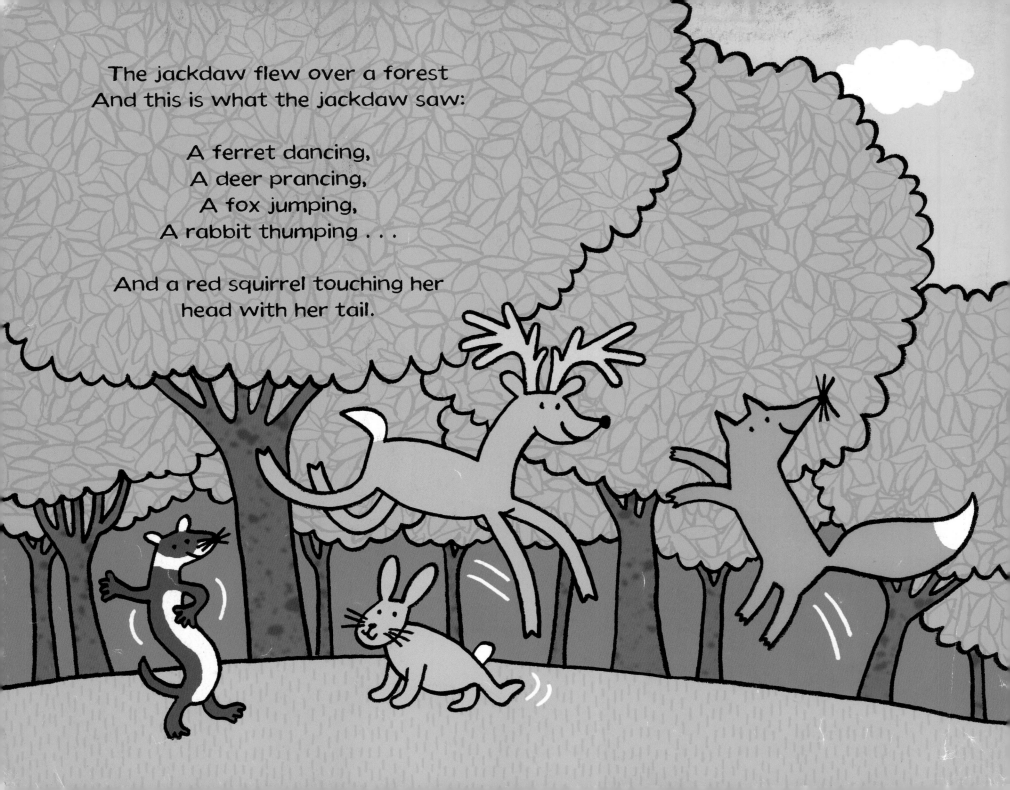

The jackdaw flew into a thundercloud,
And this is what the jackdaw saw . . .

NOTHING!

Jackdaw crashing,
Lightning flashing,
Thunder clapping,
Feathers flapping . . .

And a brown owl touching
his head with his wing.

"Why didn't they warn me?" the jackdaw cried.
"Why didn't you see them?" the owl replied.

"Octopus signing,
White horse signing,
Black cat signing,
Red squirrel signing.

Every one of them touching its head.
Danger! Danger! That's what they said."

The jackdaw flew up to the owl's branch.

Then . . .

Feathers twirling,

Wings whirling,

Eyes happy,

Feet tappy . . .

The jackdaw learned to sign with his wings.

"Come to my party!" the jackdaw signed.
Then all the animals followed behind.

The jackdaw flew back to the seaside.
Look who's there! Can you see:

Octopus drumming,
Black cat strumming,
White horse swaying,
Red squirrel playing . . .

And the jackdaw signing with his wings.

Then lots more signing
friends appeared.

"What a great party!"
everyone cheered.

Can you sign these words from the story?

Bird

Tree

Horse

Cat

Storm

Owl

Danger

Party

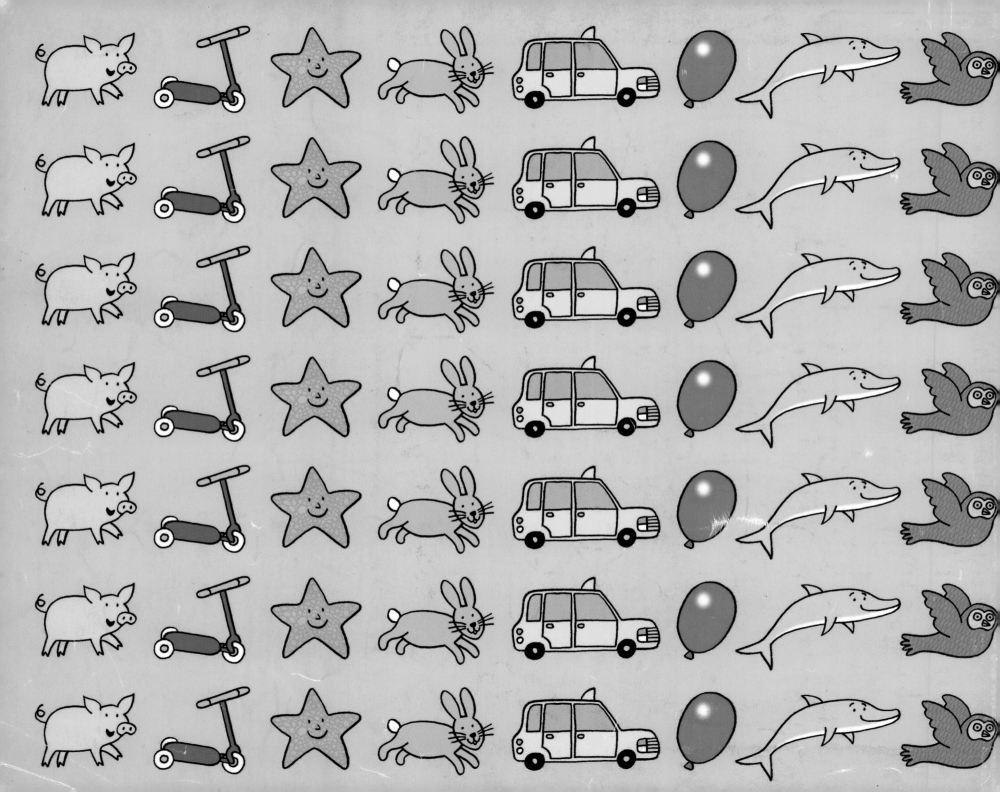

This book was written by:

Alex, Christopher, Frankie, James, Jasmine,
Jemma, Kasey, Kayleigh, Kitty, Lenka, Marcus,
Michael, Nadeem, Nazmin, Pierre, Ruky,
Sayfullah, Soemaya, Sophie and Tanvir
with Julia Donaldson

in association with

LIFE & DEAF

For all deaf children and their families - JD
For Jordanstown School - NS

First published 2015 by Macmillan Children's Books
an imprint of Pan Macmillan, a division of
Macmillan Publishers Ltd
20 New Wharf Road, London N1 9RR
Associated companies throughout the world
www.panmacmillan.com
ISBN: 978-1-4472-8083-5 (HB)
ISBN: 978-1-4472-8084-2 (PB)

Text copyright © Julia Donaldson 2015
Illustrations copyright © Nick Sharratt 2015
Moral rights asserted.

135798642

A CIP catalogue record for this book is available from the British Library.
Printed in Belgium

NOTE TO READERS:
The website address listed in this book is correct at the time of going to print. However, due to the ever-changing nature of the internet,
website addresses and content can change. The publisher cannot be held responsible for changes in website addresses or content or for
information obtained through third party websites. We strongly advise that all internet searches are supervised by an adult.